S0-BQX-400

Lust

Lust

Lascivious Love Stories and Passionate Poems

EDITED BY JOHN
AND KIRSTEN MILLER
DRAWINGS BY LORNA STOVALL

CHRONICLE BOOKS
SAN FRANCISCO

Printed in the United States of America.
Page 129 constitutes a continuation of the copyright page.

Library of Congress Cataloging–in–Publication Data
Lust: lascivious love stories and passionate poems / edited by John and Kirsten
Miller; drawings by Lorna Stovall.
p. cm.
ISBN 0-8118-0691-X (hc)
1. Lust—Literary collections.
I. Miller, John, 1959- . II. Miller Kirsten, 1963- .
PN6071.L86L87 1994
808.8'03538—dc20

93-28053
CIP

Editing and design: Big Fish Books
Composition: Jennifer Petersen, Big Fish Books

Distributed in Canada by Raincoast Books,
112 East Third Avenue, Vancouver, B.C. V5T 1C8

10 9 8 7 6 5 4 3 2 1

CHRONICLE BOOKS
275 FIFTH STREET
SAN FRANCISCO, CA 94103

I'd give you fever
If I kissed you
Fever if I held you tight
Fever—in the morning
Fever all through the night

Fever
What a lovely way to burn.

—PEGGY LEE

CONTENTS

Lust

MARIO VARGAS LLOSA

Venus, with Love and Music

HE is Venus, the Italian one, the daughter of Jupiter, the sister of Greek Aphrodite. The organ player gives her music lessons. My name is Love. Tiny, delicate, rosy, winged, I am a thousand years old and chaste as a dragonfly. The stag, the royal peacock, and the fallow deer that can be seen through the window are as alive as the pair of lovers strolling arm in arm in the shade of the promenade lined with poplars. The satyr of the fountain, however, into whose head crystalline water flows from an alabaster basin, is not alive: it is a piece of Tuscan marble modeled by a clever artist come from the South of France.

We three are alive, too, and as vivacious as the little stream that sings its way down the mountainside between the rocks or the chatter of the parrots that a trader from Africa sold to Don Rigoberto, our master. (The captive animals are now languishing in a cage in the garden.) Twilight has fallen and soon it will be night. When it comes with its lead—gray tatters, the organ will fall silent and the music teacher and I must leave so that the lord and master of everything to be seen here may enter this room to possess his lady. At that time, by our will and through our work well done, Venus will be ready to receive him and entertain him as his rank and fortune merit. That is to say, with the fire of a volcano, the sensuality of a serpent, and the hauteur of a pampered Angora cat.

The young music teacher and I are not here to enjoy ourselves but to work, though all work done wholeheartedly

and well turns, it is true, into pleasure. Our task consists
of kindling the lady's bodily joy, poking up the ashes of
each one of her five senses till they burst into flame,
and peopling her fair-haired head with filthy fan-
tasies. That is how Don Rigoberto likes to have
us hand her over to him: ardent and avid, all her
moral and religious scruples in abeyance and
her mind and body filled to overflowing with
appetites. It is an agreeable task, though not an
easy one; it requires patience, cunning, and skill
in the art of attuning the fury of instinct to the
mind's subtlety and the heart's tender affections.

    The repetitive, churchly strains of the organ
create an auspicious atmosphere. It is generally
thought that the organ, so closely associated
with the Mass and the religious hymn,
desensualizes and even disincarnates the humble
mortal bathed in its waves. A gross error; in truth,
organ music, with its obsessive languor and its soft purr,
merely disconnects the Christian from the world and

from contingency, isolating his mind so that it may turn toward something exclusive and different: God and salvation, quite true, in countless cases; but also, in many others, sin, perdition, lust, and other harsh municipal synonyms for what is expressed by that limpid word: pleasure.

The sound of the organ calms the lady and quiets her mind: a flaccid immobility not unlike ecstasy steals over her and she then half closes her eyes so as to concentrate more intently on the melody which, as it invades her, removes from her mind the preoccupations and the petty concerns of the day and drains it of everything that is not audition, pure sensation. That is how it begins. The teacher plays with an agile, self-assured, unhurried touch, in a soft, melting crescendo, choosing ambiguous compositions that discreetly transport us to austere retreats under the monastic rule of Saint Bernard, to street processions that are suddenly transformed into a pagan carnival, and thence, without transition, to the Gregorian chant of an abbey or the sung Mass of a cathedral attended by a profusion of cardinals, and finally to a promiscuous masked ball in a mansion on the outskirts of the city. Wine flows in abundance and there are suspicious movements in the leafy bowers of the garden.

A beautiful maiden, sitting in the lap of a lustful, pot-bellied old gaffer, suddenly removes her mask. And who does she turn out to be? One of the stable boys! Or the androgynous village idiot with a man's cock and a woman's tits! My lady sees this series of images because I describe them to her in her ear, in a soft, perverse voice, in time to the music. My vast knowledge translates the notes of the organ that is my accomplice into provocative shapes, colors, figures, actions. That is what I am doing now, more or less perched on her back, my smooth little face jutting out over her shoulder like a sharp-pointed prod: whispering naughty stories to her. Fictions that distract her and make her smile, fictions that shock and excite her.

The teacher cannot leave off playing the organ for a single moment: his life depends on it. Don Rigoberto has warned him: "If those bellows stop working for one moment, I

5

will know that you have yielded to the temptation to touch. I shall then plunge this dagger into your heart and throw your dead body to the dogs. We shall now find out which is stronger in you, young man: desire for my fair spouse or attachment to your life." Attachment to his life, naturally.

But as the pipes throb, he has the right to look. It is a privilege that honors and exalts him, that makes him feel himself to be a monarch or a god. He takes advantage of it with deli-cious pleasure. His glances, moreover, make my task easier and complement it, since the lady, noting the fervor and the homage rendered her by the eyes of that beardless countenance and intuiting the feverish cravings that her voluptuous white con-tours arouse in that sensitive adolescent, cannot but feel deeply touched and in the grip of concupiscent humors.

Above all, when the organ player looks at her there where his gaze is fixed. What is the young musician finding, or what is he asking in that intimate Venusian retreat? What are his virgin pupils endeavoring to penetrate? What is so powerfully magnetizing him in that triangle of transparent skin, traversed in circular paths by little blue veins like rivulets, cast

in shadow by the depilated thicket of her pubis? I
could not say; nor, I believe, could he. But there is
something there that attracts his eyes in the
late afternoon each day, with the imperious-
ness of a stroke of fate or the magic of a witch's
spell. Something like the divination that, at the foot of
the sunlit mound of Venus, in the tender cleft protected
by the rounded columns of the lady's thighs,
resilient, red, moist with the dew of her privateness,
pours forth the fountain of life and pleasure. In just a little while
now, our lord and master Don Rigoberto will bend down to
drink ambrosia from it. The organ player knows that this draft
will forever be forbidden him, since he will soon be entering the
Dominican monastery. He is a pious lad who from the tender
years of his childhood felt the call of God and whom nothing or
no one will keep from the priesthood. Even though, as he has
confessed to me, these twilight parties make him break into an
icy sweat and people his dreams with demons tricked out in a
woman's tits and buttocks, they have not undermined his
religious vocation. On the contrary: they have convinced him of

the necessity, in order to save his soul and help others save theirs, of renouncing the pomp and the carnal pleasures of this world. Perhaps he casts his eyes so pertinaciously upon the curly garden of his mistress only to prove to himself and to show God that he is capable of resisting temptations, even the most Luciferian of them: the imperishable body of our lady.

Neither she nor I have these moral dilemmas and problems of conscience. I because I am a little pagan god, and nonexistent besides, nothing more nor less than a fancy of the human imagination, and she because she is an obedient wife who reluctantly goes along with these soirees that are a prelude to the conjugal night, out of respect for her husband, who programs them down to the last detail. She is, then, a lady who bows to the will of her master, as a Christian wife should, so that, if these sensual love feasts are sinful, it is to be supposed that they will blacken only the soul of the person who, for personal pleasure, conceives them and orders them.

My lady's delicate and painstakingly constructed coiffure, with its curls, waves, flirtatious loose locks, rises and falls, and its baroque pearl adornments, is also a spectacle

orchestrated by Don Rigoberto. He gave precise instructions to
the hairdressers and holds daily inspection, like a military officer
reviewing his troops, of the array of jewels in my lady's dowry
so as to choose those that will gleam that night in her hair, circle
her throat, dangle from her translucent ears, and imprison her
fingers and wrists. "You are not you but my fantasy," she says
he whispers to her when he makes love to her. "You will not be
Lucrecia today but Venus, and today you will change from a
Peruvian woman into an Italian one and from a creature of this
earth into a goddess and a symbol."

Perhaps that is how she is, in Don Rigoberto's
elaborate imaginings. But she is nonetheless real, concrete,
as alive as a rose not plucked from the branch, or a little
songbird. Is she not a beautiful woman? Yes,
wondrously beautiful. Above all, at this
instant, when her instincts have begun
to awaken, revived by the studied alche-
my of the organ's prolonged notes, the
tremulous glances of the
musician,

and the ardent corruptions that I distill into her ear. My left
hand feels, there above her breast, how her skin has little by lit-
tle grown tense and hot. Her blood is beginning to boil. This is
the moment when she is at the full, or (to put it in scholarly
terms) has reached plenitude, what philosophers term the
absolute and alchemists transubstantiation.

The word that best sums up her body is: tumid.
Roused by my salacious fictions, everything about her
becomes curve and prominence, sinuous elevation, tempered
softness. That is the consistency that the connoisseur should
prefer in his partner at the hour of love: tender abundance that
appears to be just about to overflow yet remains firm, supple,
resilient as ripe fruit and freshly kneaded dough, that soft tex-
ture Italians call *morbidezza*, a word that sounds lustful even
when applied to bread.

Now that she is already on fire inside, her little head
phosphorescing with lubricious images, I shall scale her back
and roll about on the satiny geography of her body, tickling her
in the proper zones with my wings, and gambol about like a
happy little puppy on the warm pillow of her belly. These

affected gestures of mine make her laugh, and they kindle her body till it becomes an incandescent coal. My memory is already hearing her laugh that will be forthcoming, a laugh that drowns out the moans of the organ and makes the lips of the young music teacher drool. When she laughs, her nipples grow hard and erect, as though an invisible mouth were sucking them, and the muscles of her stomach ripple beneath the smooth skin with the scent of vanilla that suggests the rich treasure of warmths and moistures of her private parts. At that moment my turned-up nose can catch the faint odor of her secret juices, like a whiff of overripe cheese. The aroma of this amorous suppuration drives Don Rigoberto mad, and he—as she has told me—kneeling as if in prayer, absorbs it and impregnates himself with it to the point of blissful. intoxicated rapture. It is, he maintains, a more powerful aphrodisiac than all the elixirs, compounded of the nastiest substances, hawked to lovers by the sorcerers and procuresses of this city.

"As long as that is how you smell, I will

be your slave," she says that he says to her, with the loose tongue of those drunk on love.

The door will soon open and we will hear Don Rigoberto's soft footfalls on the carpet. We will soon see him appear at this bedside to ascertain whether the two of us, the music teacher and I, have been capable of bringing base reality closer to his tinseled fantasies. Hearing the lady's laughter, seeing her, breathing in the odor of her, he will take it that something more or less like that has happened. He will then make an almost imperceptible gesture of approval, which for us will be an order to take our leave.

The organ will fall silent; with a deep bow, the music teacher will make his exit by way of the orangery, and I will leap through the window and take off on my flying trapeze into the fragrant dark of the open sky.

The two of them, and the echo of their tender love bout, will remain behind in the boudoir.

SAPPHO

Poem

EER of gods he
seemeth to me, the blissful
Man who sits and gazes at thee before him,
Close beside thee sits, and in silence hears thee
Silverly speaking,

Laughing love's low laughter. Oh this, this only
Stirs the troubled heart in my breast to tremble!

For should I but see thee a little moment,

      Straight is my voice hushed;

Yea, my tongue is broken, and through and through me

'Neath the flesh impalpable fire runs tingling;

Nothing see my mine eyes, and a noise of roaring

      Waves in my ear sounds;

Sweat runs down in rivers, a tremor seizes

All my limbs, and paler than grass in autumn,

Caught by pains of menacing death, I falter,

      Lost in the love-trance.

          —translated by

          J. Addington Symonds

MILAN KUNDERA

Lightness and Weight

EN who pursue a multitude of women fit neatly into two categories. Some seek their own subjective and unchanging dream of a woman in all women. Others are prompted by a desire to possess the endless variety of the objective female world.

The obsession of the former is *lyrical:* what

they seek in women is themselves, their ideal, and since an ideal is by definition something that can never be found, they are disappointed again and again. The disappointment that propels them from woman to woman gives their incon-stancy a kind of romantic excuse, so that many sentimental women are touched by their unbridled philandering.

The obsession of the latter is *epic*, and women see nothing the least bit touching in it: the man projects no subjective ideal on women, and since everything interests him, nothing can disappoint him. This inability to be disap-pointed has something scandalous about it. The obsession of the epic womanizer strikes people as lacking in redemption (redemption by disappointment).

Because the lyrical womanizer always runs after the same type of woman, we even fail to notice when he exchanges one mistress for another. His friends perpetually cause misunderstandings by mixing up his lovers and calling them by the same name.

In pursuit of knowledge, epic womanizers (and of course Tomas belonged in their ranks) turn away from

conventional feminine beauty, of which they quickly tire,
and inevitably end up as curiosity collectors. They are
aware of this and a little ashamed of it, and to avoid causing
their friends embarrassment, they refrain from appearing in
public with their mistresses.

Tomas had been a window washer for nearly two
years when he was sent to a new customer whose bizarre
appearance struck him the moment he saw her. Though
bizarre, it was also discreet, understated, within the bounds
of the agreeably ordinary (Tomas's fascination with
curiosities had nothing in common with
Fellini's fascination with monsters):
she was very tall, quite a bit taller
than he was, and she had a deli—
cate and very long nose in a face so
unusual it was impossible to call it
attractive (everyone would
have protested!), yet (in
Tomas's eyes, at least) it could
not be called unattractive. She was

wearing slacks and a white blouse, and looked like an odd combination of giraffe, stork, and sensitive young boy.

She fixed him with a long, careful, searching stare that was not devoid of irony's intelligent sparkle. "Come in, Doctor," she said.

Although he realized that she knew who he was, he did not want to show it, and asked, "Where can I get some water?"

She opened the door to the bathroom. He saw a washbasin, bathtub, and toilet bowl; in front of bath, basin, and bowl lay miniature pink rugs.

When the woman who looked like a giraffe and a stork smiled, her eyes screwed up, and everything she said seemed full of irony or secret messages.

"The bathroom is all yours," she said. "You can do whatever your heart desires in it."

"May I have a bath?" Tomas asked.

"Do you like baths?" she asked.

He filled his pail with warm water and went into the living room. "Where would you like me to start?"

"It's up to you," she said with a shrug of the shoulders.

"May I see the windows in the other rooms?"

"So you want to have a look around?" Her smile seemed to indicate that window washing was only a caprice that did not interest her.

He went into the adjoining room. It was a bedroom with one large window, two beds pushed next to each other, and, on the wall, an autumn landscape with birches and a setting sun.

When he came back, he found an open bottle of wine and two glasses on the table. "How about a little something to keep your strength up during the big job ahead?"

"I wouldn't mind a little something, actually," said Tomas, and sat down at the table.

"You must find it interesting, seeing how people live," she said.

"I can't complain," said Tomas.

"All those wives at home alone, waiting for you."

"You mean grandmothers and mothers-in-law."

"Don't you ever miss your original profession?"

"Tell me, how did you find out about my original profession?"

"Your boss likes to boast about you," said the stork-woman.

"After all this time!" said Tomas in amazement.

"When I spoke to her on the phone about having the windows washed, she asked whether I didn't want you. She said you were a famous surgeon who'd been kicked out of the hospital. Well, naturally she piqued my curiosity."

"You have a fine sense of curiosity," he said.

"Is it so obvious?"

"Yes, in the way you use your eyes."

"And how do I use my eyes?"

"You squint. And then, the questions you ask."

"You mean you don't like to respond?"

Thanks to her, the conversation had been delightfully flirtatious from the outset. Nothing she said had any bearing on the outside world; it was all directed inward, towards themselves. And because it dealt so palpably with him and her, there was nothing simpler than to complement words with touch. Thus, when Tomas mentioned her squinting eyes, he stroked them, and she did the same to his. It was not a spontaneous reaction; she seemed to be consciously setting up a "do as I do" kind of game. And so they sat there face to face, their hands moving in stages along each other's bodies.

Not until Tomas reached her groin did she start resisting. He could not quite guess how seriously she meant it. Since much time had now passed and he was due at his next customer's in ten minutes, he stood up and told her he had to go.

Her face was red. "I have to sign the

order slip," she said.

"But I haven't done a thing," he objected.

"That's my fault." And then in a soft, innocent voice she drawled, "I suppose I'll just have to order you back and have you finish what I kept you from starting."

When Tomas refused to hand her the slip to sign, she said to him sweetly, as if asking him for a favor, "Give it to me. Please?" Then she squinted again and added, "After all, I'm not paying for it, my husband is. And you're not being paid for it, the state is. The transaction has nothing whatever to do with the two of us."

THE odd asymmetry of the woman who looked like a giraffe and a stork continued to excite his memory: the combination of the flirtatious and the gawky; the very real sexual desire offset by the ironic smile; the vulgar con-ventionality of the flat and the originality of its owner. What would she be like when they made love? Try as he might, he could not picture it. He thought of nothing else for several days.

among Czech
doctors), he had
the feeling she was
running back and forth outside the
bathroom, looking for a way to break in. When he
turned off the water and the flat was suddenly silent,
he felt he was being watched. He was nearly certain
that there was a peephole somewhere in the bath-
room door and that her beautiful eye was squinting
through it.

He went off in the best of moods, trying to fix her
essence in his memory, to reduce that memory to a
chemical formula capable of defining her uniqueness
(her millionth part dissimilarity). The result was a
formula consisting of three givens:

1) clumsiness with ardor,

2) the frightened face of one who has lost her equi-
librium and is falling, and,

3) legs raised in the air like the arms of a soldier
surrendering to a pointed gun.

pointed at him.

Clumsiness combined with ardor, ardor with clumsiness they excited Tomas utterly. He made love to her for a very long time, constantly scanning her red-blotched face for that frightened expression of a woman whom someone has tripped and who is falling, the inimitable expression that moments earlier had con- veyed excitement to his brain.

Then he went to wash in the bathroom. She fol- lowed him in and gave him long-drawn-out explanations of where the soap was and where the sponge was and how to turn on the hot water. He was surprised that she went into such detail over such simple matters. At last he had to tell her that he understood everything perfectly, and motioned to her to leave him alone in the bathroom.

"Won't you let me stay and watch?" she begged.

At last he managed to get her out. As he washed and urinated into the washbasin (standard procedure

women's bodies. Hers was unusually prominent, evoking
the long digestive tract that ended there with a slight pro-
trusion. Fingering her strong, healthy orb, that most
splendid of rings called by doctors the sphincter, he sud-
denly felt her fingers on the corresponding part of his own
anatomy. She was mimicking his moves with the precision
of a mirror.

Even though, as I have pointed out, he had known
approximately two hundred women (plus the considerable
lot that had accrued during his days as a window washer),
he had yet to be faced with a woman who was taller than he
was, squinted at him, and fingered his anus. To overcome
his embarrassment he forced her down on the bed.

So precipitous was his move that he caught her
off guard. As her towering frame fell on its back, he
caught among the red blotches on her face the frightened
expression of equilibrium lost. Now that he was standing
over her, he grabbed her under the knees and lifted her
slightly parted legs in the air, so that they suddenly looked
like the raised arms of a soldier surrendering to a gun

The next
time he answered
her summons, the wine
and two glasses stood waiting on the
table. And this time everything went like clockwork.
Before long, they were standing face to face in the bed-
room (where the sun was setting on the birches in the
painting) and kissing. But when he gave her his stan-
dard "Strip!" command, she not only failed to comply
but counter-commanded, "No, you first!"

Unaccustomed to such a response, he was
somewhat taken aback. She started to open his fly.
After ordering "Strip!" several more times (with
comic failure), he was forced to accept a compro-
mise. According to the rules of the game she had set up
during his last visit ("do as I do"), she took off his
trousers, he took off her skirt, and then she took off his
shirt, he her blouse, until at last they stood there naked.
He placed his hand on her moist genitals, then moved his
fingers along to the anus, the spot he loved most in all

Going over them, he felt the joy of having acquired yet another piece of the world, of having taken his imaginary scalpel and snipped yet another strip off the infinite canvas of the universe.

JAYADEVA

Gitagovinda
Careless Krishna

SWEET

notes from his alluring flute echo nectar from his
lips.
His restless eyes glance, his head sways, ear–
rings play at his cheeks.
My heart recalls Hari here in his love
dance,

Playing seductively, laughing, mocking me.

A circle of peacock plumes caressed by moonlight
crowns his hair.
A rainbow colors the fine cloth on his cloud—
dark body.
My heart recalls Hari here in his love dance,
Playing seductively, laughing, mocking me.

Kissing mouths of round—hipped cowherd girls
whets his lust.
Brilliant smiles flash from the ruby—red buds of his
sweet lips.
My heart recalls Hari here in his love dance,
Playing seductively, laughing, mocking me.

Vines of his great throbbing arms circle a thousand
cowherdesses.
Jewel rays from his hands and feet and chest break
the dark night.

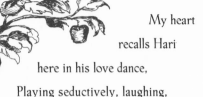

My heart
recalls Hari
here in his love dance,
Playing seductively, laughing,
mocking me.

His sandalpaste browmark outshines the moon in a
mass of clouds.
His cruel heart is a hard door bruising circles of
swelling breasts.
My heart recalls Hari here in his love dance,
Playing seductively, laughing, mocking me.

Jeweled earrings in sea−serpent form adorn his
sublime cheeks.
His trailing yellow cloth is a retinue of sages, gods,
and spirits.
My heart recalls Hari here in his love dance,
Playing seductively, laughing, mocking me.

Meeting me under a flowering tree, he calms my fear of
dark time,
Delighting me deeply by quickly glancing looks at my heart.
 My heart recalls Hari here in his love dance,
 Playing seductively, laughing, mocking me.

Jayadeva's song evokes an image of Madhu's beautiful foe
Fit for worthy men who keep the memory of Hari's feet.
 My heart recalls Hari here in his love dance,
 Playing seductively, laughing, mocking me.

Indolent Krishna

SEEING Rādhā in her retreat of vines,
Powerless to leave, impassioned too long,
Her friend described her state
While Krishna lay helpless with love.

In her loneliness she sees you everywhere
Drinking springflower honey from other lips.
  Lord Hari,
  Rādhā suffers in her retreat.

Rushing in her haste to meet you,
She stumbles after a few steps and falls.
  Lord Hari,
  Rādhā suffers in her retreat.

Weaving bracelets from supple lotus shoots
As symbols of your skillful love, she keeps alive.
  Lord Hari,
  Rādhā suffers in her retreat.

  Staring at her ornaments' natural grace,
  She fancies, "I am Krishna, Madhu's foe."
  Lord Hari,
   Rādhā suffers in her retreat.

"Why won't Hari
come quickly to
meet me?"

She incessantly asks her friend.
> Lord Hari,
> Rādhā suffers in her retreat.

She embraces, she kisses cloud–like forms
Of the vast dark night. "Hari has come," she says.
> Lord Hari,
> Rādhā suffers in her retreat.

While you idle here, modesty abandons her,
She laments, sobs as she waits to love you.
> Lord Hari,
> Rādhā suffers in her retreat.

May poet Jayadeva's song
Bring joy to sensitive men!

Lord Hari,

Rādhā suffers in her retreat.

Her body bristling with longing,

Her breath sucking in words of confusion,

Her voice cracking in deep cold fear—

Obsessed by intense thoughts of passion,

Rādhā sinks in a sea of erotic mood,

Clinging to you in her meditation, cheat!

She ornaments her limbs

When a leaf quivers or a feather falls.

Suspecting your coming,

She spreads out the bed

And waits long in meditation.

Making her bed of ornaments and fantasies,

She evokes a hundred details of you

In her own graceful play.

But the frail girl will not survive

Tonight without you

Cunning Krishna

HIS eyes flirt like blue night lilies in the wind.
The bed of tender shoots won't burn her.
> Wildflower-garlanded Krishna
> Caresses her, friend.

His soft mouth moves like an open lotus.
Arrows of love won't wound her.
> Wildflower-garlanded Krishna
> Caresses her, friend.

His mellow speech is elixir of honey.
Sandal mountain winds won't scorch her.
> Wildflower-garlanded Krishna
> Caresses her, friend.

His hands and feet gleam like hibiscus blossoms.

Cold moon rays won't make her writhe.
  Wildflower-garlanded Krishna
      Caresses her, friend.

His color deepens like rain-heavy thunderheads.
  Long desertion won't tear at her heart.
      Wildflower-garlanded Krishna
          Caresses her, friend.

His bright cloth shines gold on black touchstone.
  Her servants' teasing won't make her sigh.
      Wildflower-garlanded Krishna
          Caresses her, friend.

His tender youth touches all creatures.
  She won't feel the pain of terrible pity.
      Wildflower-garlanded Krishna
          Caresses her, friend.

Through words that Jayadeva sings

May Hari possess your heart!
    Wildflower–garlanded Krishna
    Caresses her, friend.

Sandalwood mountain wind,
As you blow southern breezes
To spread the bliss of love,
Soothe me! End the paradox!
Lifebreath of the world,
If you bring me Madhava
For a moment,
You may take my life!

Friends are hostile,
Cool wind is like fire,
Moon nectar is poison,
Krishna torments me in my heart.
But even when he is cruel
I am forced to take him back.
Women with night–lily eyes feel love

In a paradox of passion–bound infinity.

Command my torment, sandal mountain wind!

Take my lifebreath with arrows, Love!

I will not go home for refuge again!

Jumna river, sister of Death,

Why should you bekind?

Drown my limbs with waves!

Let my body's burning be quenched!

ITALO CALVINO

The Loves of the Tortoises

HERE are two tortoises on the patio: a male and a female. *Zlak! Zlak!* Their shells strike each other. It is their mating season.

The male pushes the female sideways, all around the edge of the paving. The female seems to resist his attack, or at least she opposes it with inert immobility. The male is smaller and more active; he seems younger. He tries repeatedly to mount her, from behind, but the back of her shell is steep and he slides off.

Now he must have succeeded in achieving the right position: he thrusts with rhythmic, cadenced strokes; at every thrust he emits a kind of gasp, almost a cry. The female has her foreclaws flattened against the ground, enabling her to raise her hind part. The male scratches his foreclaws on her shell, his neck stuck out, his mouth gaping. The problem with these shells is that there's no way to get a hold; in fact the claws can find no purchase.

Now she escapes him; he pursues her. Not that she is faster or particularly deter-mined to run away: to restrain her he gives her some nips on a leg, always the same one. She does not rebel. Every time she stops, the male tries to mount her; but she takes a little step forward and he topples off, slamming his member on the ground. This member is fairly long, hooked in a way that apparently makes it possible for him to reach her even though the thickness of the shells and their awkward positioning separates them. So there is no telling how many of these attacks achieve their purpose or how many fail, or how many are theater, play-acting.

It is summer; the patio is bare, except for one green jasmine in a corner. The courtship consists of making so many turns around the little patch of grass, with pursuits and flights and skirmishing not of the claws but of the shells, which strike in a dull clicking. The female tries to find refuge among the stalks of the jasmine; she believes—or wants to make others believe—that she does this to hide; but actually this is the surest way to remain blocked by the male, held immobile with no avenue of escape. Now he has most likely managed to introduce his member properly; but this time they are both completely still, silent.

The sensations of the pair of mating tortoises are something Mr. Palomar cannot imagine. He observes them with a cold attention, as if they were two machines: two electronic tortoises programmed to mate. What does eros become if there are plates of bone or horny scales in the place of skin? But what we call eros—is it perhaps only a program of our corporeal bodies, more complicated because the memory receives messages from every cell of the skin, from every molecule of our tissues, and multiplies them and combines them with the impulses transmitted by our eyesight and with those aroused by the imagination? The difference lies only in the number of circuits involved: from our receptors billions of wires extend, linked with the computer of feelings, conditionings, the ties between one person and another. . . . Eros is a program that unfolds in the electronic clusters of the mind, but the mind is also skin: skin touched, seen, remembered. And what about the tortoises, enclosed in their insensitive casing? The poverty of their sensorial stimuli perhaps drives them to a concentrated, intense mental life, leads them to a crystalline inner awareness. . . . Perhaps the eros of tortoises obeys absolute spiritual laws, whereas we are prisoners of a machinery whose functioning remains unknown to us, prone to clog-

ging up, stalling,
exploding in
uncontrolled
automatisms. . . .

Do the tortoises understand themselves
anybetter? After about ten minutes of mating, the two
shells separate. She ahead, he behind, they resume
their circling of the grass. Now the male remains
more distanced; every now and then he scratches his
claw against her shell, he climbs on her for a little,
but without much conviction. They go back under the
jasmine. He gives her a nip or two on a leg, always
in the same place.

The Prime of Life

 HAD

surrendered my virginity with glad abandon: when heart, head, and body are all in unison, there is high delight to be had from the physical expression of that oneness. At first I had experienced nothing but pleasure, which matched my natural optimism and was balm to my pride. But very soon circumstances forced me into awareness of something which I had uneasily foreseen when I was twenty: simple physical desire. I knew nothing of such an appetite: I had never in my life suffered from hunger, or thirst, or lack of sleep. Now, suddenly, I fell a victim to it. I was separated from Sartre for days or even weeks at a time. On our Sundays in Tours we were too shy to go up to a hotel bedroom in broad daylight; and besides, I would not have love-making take on the appearance of a concerted enterprise. I was all for liberty, but dead set against deliberation. I refused to admit either that one could yield to desires against one's will, or the possibility of organizing one's pleasures in cold blood. The pleasures of love-making should be as unforeseen and irresistible as the surge of the sea or a peach tree breaking into blossom. I could not have explained why, but the idea of any discrepancy between my physical emotions and my conscious will I found alarming in the extreme: and it was precisely this split that in fact took place. My body had its own whims, and I was powerless to control them; their violence overrode all my defenses. I found out that missing a person physically is

not a mere matter of nostalgia, but an actual *pain.* From the
roots of my hair to the soles of my feet a poisoned shirt was
woven across my body. I hated suffering; I hated the thought
that this suffering was born of my blood, that I was involved
in it; I even went so far as to hate the very pulsing of the
blood through my veins. Every morning in the Métro, still
numb with sleep, I would stare at my fellow travelers,
wondering if they too were familiar with this torture, and
how it was that no book I knew had ever described its full
agony. Gradually the poisoned shirt would dissolve, and
I would feel the fresh morning air caressing my closed
eyelids. But by nightfall my obsession would rouse
itself once more, and thousands of ants would crawl
across my lips: the mirror showed me bursting
with health, but a hidden disease was rotting the
marrow in my very bones.

A shameful disease, too. I had
emancipated myself just far enough
from my puritanical upbring-
ing to be

able to take unconstrained pleasure in my own body, but not so far that I could allow it to cause me any inconvenience. Starved of its sustenance, it begged and pleaded with me: I found it repulsive. I was forced to admit a truth that I had been doing my best to conceal ever since my adolescence: my physical appetites were greater than I wanted them to be. In the feverish caresses and love-making that bound me to the man of my choice I could discern the movements of my heart, my freedom as an individual. But that mood of solitary, languorous excitement cried out for anyone, regardless. In the night train from Tours to Paris the touch of an anonymous hand along my leg could arouse feelings— against my conscious will—of quite shattering intensity. I said nothing about these shameful incidents. Now that I had embarked on our policy of absolute frankness, this reticence was, I felt, a kind of touchstone. If I dared not confess such things, it was because they were by definition unavowable. By driving me to such secrecy my body became a stumbling block rather than a bond of union between us, and I felt a burning resentment against it.

Though I had available a whole set of moral precedents which encouraged me to take sexual encounters lightly, I found that my personal experience gave them the lie. I was too convinced a materialist to distinguish, as Alain and his followers did, between body and mind, conceding each its due.

To judge from my own case, the mind did *not* exist in isolation from the body, and my body compromised me completely. I might well have inclined toward Claudel's type of sublimation, and in particular toward that naturalistic optimism which claims to reconcile the rational and instinctive elements in man; but the truth was that for me, at any rate, this "reconciliation" simply did not work. My reason could not come to terms with my tyrannical desires. I learned with my body that humanity does *not* subsist in the calm light of the Good; men suffer the dumb, futile, cruel agonies of defenseless beasts. The face of the earth must have been hellish indeed to judge by the dark and lurid desires that, from time to time, struck me with the force of a thunderbolt.

PASOLINI

ROMAN POEMS

Toward the Caracalla Baths

OING toward

the Caracalla Baths

young friends

on Rumi or Ducati bikes

with male modesty and male immodesty

indifferently hiding or revealing

in the warm folds of their trousers

5 0

the secret of their erections . . .
With wavy hair
in youthful colored sweaters
they cleave the night,
in an endless carrousel,
they invade the night,
splendid masters of the night . . .

Going toward the Caracalla Baths
with bare chest, as if upon
his native Apennine slopes
among sheep trails
for centuries smelling
of animals and holy ashes
from Berber countries—
already impure, under his dusty rough beret,
hands in his pockets—
the shepherd migrated
when he was eleven,
and now here he is,

jesting scoundrel with his Roman smile
still warm with red sage, figs and olives . ...

Going toward the Caracalla Baths,
the old paterfamilias, unemployed,
reduced by ferocious Frascati
to a blissful dumb beast
with the scrap-iron chassis
of his broken body wheezing,
his clothes a sack containing
a back slightly hunched
and two thighs covered with scabs,
rough trousers flapping
under the pockets of his jacket
    full of crumpled paper bags.
        The face laughs:
        under the jaws, the creaking bones
        chewing words,
            he laughs to himself,
                            then stops

and rolls an old butt,

his carcass in which all youth

remains in bloom,

like a bonfire

in an old basket or basin:

He never dies who was never born.

Going toward the Caracalla Baths . . .

Sex, Consolation for Misery

Sex, consolation for misery!

The whore is queen, her throne a ruin,

her land a piece of shitty field,

her sceptre a purse of red patent leather:

she barks in the night,

dirty and ferocious as an ancient mother:

she defends her possessions and her life.

The pimps swarming around

bloated and beat

with their Brindisi or Slavic moustaches

are leaders, rulers:

in the dark they make their hundred *lire* deals,

winking in silence, exchanging passwords:

the world, excluded, remains silent

about those who have excluded themselves,

silent carcasses of predators.

But from the world's trash

a new world is born,

new laws are born

in which honor is dishonor,

a ferocious nobility and power is born

in the piles of hovels

in the open spaces

where one thinks the city ends

and where instead it begins again, hostile,

begins again a thousand times,

with bridges and labyrinths,
foundations and diggings,
behind a surge of skyscrapers
covering whole horizons.

In the ease of love
the wretch feels himself a man,
builds up faith in life,
and ends despising all who have a different life.
The sons throw themselves into adventure
secure in a world which fears them and their sex.
Their piety is in being pitiless,
their strength in their lightness,
their hope in having no hope.

Triumph of the Might

THE pile of orange ruins
which the night stains
with the fresh color of tartar,
grassgrown ramparts of light pumice
reaching to the sky,
and even emptier down below
the Baths of Caracalla
open wide to the burning moon
on the grassless fields and trampled bushes
in the still dusk:
　all fades and grows dim
　　　　among Caravaggio colonnades of dust
　　　　and silver fans which
　　　　the little disk of the country moon
　　　　carves in iridescent puffs of smoke.
　　　　　　From that big sky

"clients" come down like heavy
 shadows,
soldiers from Puglia or Lombardy,
kids from Trastevere, alone, in gangs.
In the low square
they stop where the women
burnt-out and loose
like rags aflutter in the evening air
redden and yell
like sordid little sisters,
like innocent old women and mothers,
in the very heart of the surrounding city
freighted with the rasping of trams
and meshes of light,
in their ninth circle of Hell
they arouse the trousers stiff with dust
that throw themselves into a despicable trot
over the garbage and livid dew.

JOHN DONNE

To His Mistress Going to Bed

OME, Madam,
come, all rest my powers defy,
Until I labour, I in labour lie.
The foe oft-times, having the foe in sight,
Is tired with standing, though they never fight.
Off with that girdle, like heaven's zone glistering,
But a far fairer world encompassing.
Unpin that spangled breastplate which you wear,

That th' eyes
of busy fools
may be stopped there:
Unlace yourself, for that harmonious chime,
Tells me from you that now it's your bed time.
Off with that happy busk, which I envy,
That still can be, and still can stand so nigh.
Your gown's going off, such beauteous
state reveals,
As when from flowery meads th'hill's
shadow steals.

     Off with your wiry coronet and show
The hairy diadem which on you doth grow.
Off with those shoes and then safely tread
In this love's hallowed temple, this soft bed.
In such white robes, heaven's angels used to be
Received by men; thou Angel bring'st with thee
A heaven like Mahomet's Paradise; and though
Ill spirits walk in white, we easily know,
By this these Angels from an evil sprite;
They set our hairs, but these the flesh upright.

     Licence my roving hands, and let them go,

Behind, before, above, between, below.

Oh my America! my new-foundland,

My kingdom, safeliest when with one man manned,

My mine of precious stones, my Empery,

How blessed am I in this discovering thee!

To enter in these bonds is to be free

Then where my hand is set my seal shall be.

     Full nakedness, all joys are due to thee,

As souls unbodied, bodies unclothed must be

To taste whole joys. Gems which you women use

Are as Atlanta's balls, cast in men's views,

  That when a fool's eye lighteth on a gem,

   His earthly soul may covet theirs not them.

    Like pictures, or like books' gay coverings made

     For lay-men, are all women thus arrayed;

      Themselves are mystic books, which only we

        Whom their imputed grace will dignify

          Must see revealed. Then since that

          I may know,

          As liberally as to a midwife show

            Thyself, cast all, yea this white

               linen hence.

Here is no penance, much less innocence.

    To teach thee, I am naked first. Why then
What need'st thou have more covering than a man.

VLADIMIR NABOKOV

Lolita

 WANT my
learned readers to participate in the scene I am about to
replay; I want them to examine its every detail and see
for themselves how careful, how chaste, the whole
wine–sweet event is if viewed with what my lawyer
has called, in a private talk we have had, "impartial
sympathy." So let us get started. I have a

difficult job before me.

Main character: Humbert the Hummer. Time: Sunday morning in June. Place: sunlit living room. Props: old, candy-striped davenport, magazines, phonograph, Mexican knickknacks (the late Mr. Harold E. Haze—God bless the good—man had engendered my darling at the siesta hour in a blue-washed room, on a honeymoon trip to Vera Cruz, and mementoes, among these Dolores, were all over the place). She wore that day a pretty print dress that I had seen on her once before, ample in the skirt, tight in the bodice, short-sleeved, pink, checkered with darker pink, and, to complete the color scheme, she had painted her lips and was holding in her hollowed hands a beautiful, banal, Eden-red apple. She was not shod, however, for church. And her white Sunday purse lay discarded near the phonograph.

My heart beat like a drum as she sat down, cool skirt ballooning, subsiding, on the sofa next to me, and played with her glossy fruit. She tossed it up into the sun-dusted air, and caught it—it made a cupped polished *plop*.

Humbert Humbert intercepted the apple.

"Give it back," she pleaded, showing the marbled flush of her palms. I produced Delicious. She grasped it and bit into it, and my heart was like snow under thin crimson skin, and with the monkeyish nimbleness that was so typical of that American nymphet, she snatched out of my abstract grip the magazine I had opened (pity no film has recorded the curious pattern, the monogrammic linkage of our simultaneous or overlapping moves). Rapidly, hardly hampered by the disfigured apple she held, Lo flipped violently through the pages in search of something she wished Humbert to see. Found it at last. I faked interest by bringing my head so close that her hair touched my temple and her arm brushed my cheek as she wiped her lips with her wrist. Because of the burnished mist through which I peered at the picture, I was slow in reacting to it, and her bare knees rubbed and knocked impatiently against each other. Dimly there came into view: a surrealist painter relaxing, supine, on a beach, and near him, likewise supine, a plaster replica of the Venus di Milo, half-buried in sand. Picture of the Week, said the legend. I whisked the whole obscene thing away. Next moment, in a sham effort to retrieve it, she was all over me. Caught her by her thin knobby wrist. The magazine escaped to the floor like a flustered fowl. She twisted herself free, recoiled, and lay back in the right-hand corner of the davenport. Then, with perfect simplicity, the impudent child extended her legs across my lap.

By this time I was in a state of excitement border-ing on insanity; but I also had the cunning of the insane. Sitting there, on the sofa, I managed to attune, by a series of stealthy movements, my masked lust to her guileless limbs. It was no easy matter to divert the little maiden's attention while I performed the obscure adjustments necessary for the success of the trick. Talking fast, lagging behind my own breath, catching up with it, mimicking a sudden toothache to explain the breaks in my patter—and all the while keeping a maniac's inner eye on my distant golden goal, I cautiously

increased the
magic friction
that was doing
away, in an illusional, if not fac-
tual sense, with the physically irremovable, but
psychologically very friable texture of the material
divide (pajamas and robe) between the weight of
two sunburnt legs, resting athwart my lap, and the
hidden tumor of an unspeakable passion. Having, in
the course of my patter, hit upon something nicely
mechanical, I recited, garbling them slightly, the
words of a foolish song that was then popular—O
my Carmen, my little Carmen, something, some-
thing, those something nights, and the stars, and the
cars, and the bars, and the barmen; I kept repeating this
automatic stuff and holding her under its special spell (spe-
cial because of the garbling), and all the while I was mortally
afraid that some act of God might interrupt me, might
remove the golden load in the sensation of which all my
being seemed concentrated, and this anxiety forced me to

work, for the first minute or so, more hastily than was con-
sensual with deliberately modulated enjoyment. The stars
that sparkled, and the cars that parkled, and the bars, and
the barmen, were presently taken over by her; her voice
stole and corrected the tune I had been mutilating. She was
musical and apple-sweet. Her legs twitched a little as they
lay across my live lap; I stroked them; there she lolled in
the right-hand corner, almost asprawl, Lola the bobby-
soxer, devouring her immemorial fruit, singing through
its juice, losing her slipper, rubbing the heel of her
slipperless foot in its sloppy anklet, against the pile of
old magazines heaped on my left on the sofa—and
every movement she made, every shuffle and ripple,
helped me to conceal and improve the secret
system of tactile correspondence
between beast and beauty—
between my gagged, bursting beast
and the beauty of her dimpled body in
its innocent cotton
frock.

Under my glancing finger tips I felt the minute
hairs bristle ever so slightly along her shins. I lost myself
in the pungent but healthy heat which like summer haze
hung about little Haze. Let her stay, let her stay . . . As
she strained to chuck the core of her abolished apple into
the fender, her young weight, her shameless innocent
shanks and round bottom, shifted in my tense, tortured,
surreptitiously laboring lap; and all of a sudden a mysteri-
ous change came over my senses. I entered a plane of
being where nothing mattered, save the infusion of joy
brewed within my body. What had begun as a delicious
distension of my innermost roots became a glowing tingle
which *now* had reached that state of absolute security,
confidence and reliance not found elsewhere in conscious
life. With the deep hot sweetness thus established and well
on its way to the ultimate convulsion, I felt I could slow
down in order to prolong the glow. Lolita had been safely
solipsized. The implied sun pulsated in the supplied
poplars; we were fantastically and divinely alone. I
watched her, rosy, gold-dusted, beyond the veil of my

controlled delight, unaware of it, alien to it, and the sun
was on her lips, and her lips were apparently still forming
the words of the Carmen-barmen ditty that no longer
reached my consciousness. Everything was now ready.
The nerves of pleasure had been laid bare. The corpuscles
of Krauze were entering the phase of frenzy. The least
pressure would suffice to set all paradise loose. I had
ceased to be Humbert the Hound, the sad-eyed degenerate
cur clasping the boot that would presently kick him away.
I was above the tribulations of ridicule, beyond the possi-
bilities of retribution. In my self-made seraglio, I was a
radiant and robust Turk, deliberately, in the full con-
sciousness of his freedom, postponing the moment of actu-
ally enjoying the youngest and frailest of his slaves.
Suspended on the brink of that voluptuous abyss (a nicety
of physiological equipoise comparable to certain
techniques in the arts) I kept repeating chance
words after her—barmen, alarmin', my charmin'
my carmen, ahmen, ahahamen—as one talking and
laughing in his sleep while my happy hand crept up

her sunny leg as far as the shadow of decency allowed. The day before she had collided with a heavy chest in the hall and—"Look, look!"—I gasped—"look what you've done, what you've done to yourself, ah, look"; for there was, I swear, a yellowish-violet bruise on her lovely nymphet thigh which my huge hairy hand massaged and slowly enveloped—and because of her very perfunctory underthings, there seemed to be nothing to prevent my muscular thumb from reaching the hot hollow of her groin—just as you might tickle and caress a giggling child—just that—and "Oh it's nothing at all," she cried with a sudden shrill note in her voice, and she wriggled, and squirmed, and threw her head back, and her teeth rested on her glistening underlip as she half turned away, and my moaning mouth, gentlemen of the jury, almost reached her bare neck, while I crushed out against her left buttock the last throb of the longest ecstasy man or monster had ever known.

Immediately afterward (as if we had been struggling and now my grip had eased) she rolled off the sofa and

jumped to her feet—to her foot, rather—in order to attend
to the formidably loud telephone that may have been ringing
for ages as far as I was concerned. There she stood and
blinked, cheeks aflame, hair awry, her eyes passing over me
as lightly as they did over the furniture, as she listened or
spoke (to her mother who was telling her to come to lunch
with her at the Chatfields—neither Lo nor Hum knew yet
what busybody Haze was plotting), she kept tapping the
edge of the table with the slipper she held in her hand.
Blessed be the Lord, she had noticed nothing!

    With a handkerchief of multicolored silk, on which
her listening eyes rested in passing, I wiped the sweat
off my forehead, and, immersed in a euphoria of
release, rearranged my royal robes. She was still at
the telephone, haggling with her mother
(wanted to be fetched by car, my little Carmen)
when, singing louder and louder, I swept up the
stairs and set a deluge of steaming water roaring into
the tub.

CHARLES BAUDELAIRE

Afternoon Song

HOUGH
your wicked eyebrows call

Your nature into question

(Unangelic's their suggestion,

Witch whose eyes enthrall).

I adore you still—

O foolish, terrible emotion—
Kneeling in devotion
As a priest to his idol will.

Your undone braids conceal
Desert, forest scents:
In your exotic countenance
Lie secrets unrevealed.

Over your flesh perfume drifts
Like incense 'round a censer:
Tantalizing dispenser
Of evening's ardent gifts.

No philtres could compete
With your potent idleness:
You've mastered the caress
That raises dead men to their feet.

Your hips themselves are romanced
By your back and by your breasts:
Even the cushions are impressed
By your languid dalliance.

Now and then, your appetite's
Uncontrolled, unassuaged:
Mysteriously enraged,
You kiss me and you bite.

Dark one. I am torn
By your savage, mocking ways,
Then, soft as the moon, your gaze
Sees my tortured heart reborn.

Beneath your satin shoe,
Beneath your charming silken foot.
My greatest joy I put
My genius and destiny, too.

You bring my spirit back,
Bringer of the light.
Exploding color in the night
Of my Siberia so black.

—Translated by Randall Koral and Ruth Marshall

The Vampire Lestat

 T was thirst
that awakened me.

And I knew at once where I was, and what I
was, too.

There were no sweet mortal dreams of chilled
white wine or the fresh green grass beneath the apple
trees in my father's orchard.

In the narrow darkness of the stone coffin, I felt of my fangs with my fingers and found them dangerously long and keen as little knife blades.

And a mortal was in the tower, and though he hadn't reached the door of the outer chamber I could *hear* his thoughts.

I *heard* his consternation when he discovered the door to the stairs unlocked. That had never happened before. I heard his fear as he discovered the burnt timbers on the floor and called out "Master." A servant was what he was, and a somewhat treacherous one at that.

It fascinated me, this soundless hearing of his mind, but something else was disturbing me. It was his scent!

I lifted the stone lid of the sarcophagus and climbed out. The scent was faint but it was almost irre-sistible. It was the musky smell of the first whore in whose bed I had spent my passion. It was the roasted venison after days and days of starvation in winter. It was new wine, or fresh apples, or water roaring over a cliff's edge on a hot day when I reached out to gulp it in handfuls.

Only it was immeasurably richer than that, this scent, and the appetite that wanted it was infinitely keener and more simple.

I moved through the secret tunnel like a creature swimming through the darkness and, pushing out the stone in the outer chamber, rose to my feet.

There stood the mortal, staring at me, his face pale with shock.

An old, withered man he was, and by some indefinable tangle of considerations in his mind, I knew he was a stable master and a coachman. But the hearing of this was maddeningly imprecise.

Then the immediate malice he felt towards me came like the heat of a stove. And there was no misunderstanding that. His eyes raced over my face and form. The hatred boiled, crested. It was he who had

procured the fine clothes I wore. He who had tended the
unfortunates in the dungeon while they had lived. And why,
he demanded in silent outrage, was I not there?

This made me love him very much, as you can
imagine. I could have crushed him to death in my bare
hands for this.

"The master!" he said desperately. "Where is he?
Master!"

But what did he think the master was? A sorcerer
of some king, that was what he thought. And now I had the
power. In sum, he didn't know anything that would be of
use to me.

But as I comprehended all this, as I drank it up
from his mind, quite against his will, I was becoming
entranced with the veins in his face and in his hands. And
that smell was intoxicating me.

I could feel the dim throbbing of his heart, and
then I could taste his blood, just what it would be like, and
there came to me some full-blown sense of it, rich and hot
as it filled me.

"The master's gone, burned in the fire," I murmured, hearing a strong monotone coming from myself. I moved slowly towards him.

He glanced at the blackened floor. He looked up at the blackened ceiling. "No, this is a lie," he said. He was outraged, and his anger pulsed like a light in my eye. I felt the bitterness of his mind and its desperate reasoning.

Ah, but that living flesh could look like this! I was in the grip of remorseless appetite.

And he knew it. In some wild and unreasoning way, he sensed it; and throwing me one last malevolent glance he ran for the stairway.

Immediately I caught him. In fact, I enjoyed catching him, so simple it was. One instant I was willing myself to reach out and close the distance between us. The next I had him helpless in my hands, holding him off the floor so that his feet swung free, straining to kick me.

I held him as easily as a powerful man might hold a child, that was the proportion. His mind was a jumble of frantic thoughts, and he seemed unable to decide

upon any course to
save himself.

But the faint humming of
these thoughts was being obliterated by the vision he
presented to me.

His eyes weren't the portals of his soul any-
more. They were gelatinous orbs whose colors tantalized
me. And his body was nothing but a writhing morsel of hot
flesh and blood, that I must have or die without.

It horrified me that this food should be alive, that
delicious blood should flow through these struggling arms
and fingers, and then it seemed perfect that it should. He
was what he was, and I was what I was, and I was going
to feast upon him.

I pulled him to my lips. I tore the bulging artery
in his neck. The blood hit the roof of my mouth. I gave a
little cry as I crushed him against me. It wasn't the burn-
ing fluid the master's blood had been, not that lovely elixir
I had drunk from the stones of the dungeon. No, that had
been light itself made liquid. Rather this was a thousand

times more luscious, tasting of the thick human heart that pumped it, the very essence of that hot, almost smoky scent.

I could feel my shoulders rising, my fingers biting deeper into his flesh, and almost a humming sound rising out of me. No vision but that of his tiny gasping soul, but a swoon so powerful that he himself, what he was, had no part in it.

It was with all my will that, before the final moment, I forced him away. How I wanted to feel his heart stop. How I wanted to feel the beats slow and cease and know I *possessed* him.

But I didn't dare.

He slipped heavily from my arms, his limbs sprawling out on the stones, the whites of his eyes showing beneath his half-closed eyelids.

And I found myself unable to turn away from his death, mutely fascinated by it. Not the smallest detail must escape me. I heard his breath give out, I saw the body relax into death without a struggle.

The blood warmed me. I felt it beating in my veins. My face was hot against the palms of my hands, and my vision had grown powerfully sharp. I felt strong beyond all imagining.

PABLO NERUDA

Drunk with Pines

RUNK with
pines and long kisses,

like summer I steer the fast sail of the
roses,

bent towards the death of the thin day,

stuck into my solid marine madness.

Pale and lashed to my ravenous water,
I cruise in the sour smell of the naked climate,
still dressed in grey and bitter sounds
and a sad crest of abandoned spray.

Hardened by passions, I go mounted on my one wave,
lunar, solar, burning and cold, all at once,
becalmed in the throat of the fortunate isles
that are white and sweet as cool hips.

In the moist night my garment of kisses trembles
charged to insanity with electric currents,
heroically divided into dreams
and intoxicating roses practising on me.

Upstream, in the midst of the outer waves,
your parallel body yields to my arms
like a fish infinitely fastened to my soul,
quick and slow, in the energy under the sky.

Delta of Venus

LENA dreamed of Pierre and Bijou. The full-fleshed Bijou, the whore, the animal, the lioness; a luxuriant goddess of abundance, her flesh a bed of sensuality—every pore and curve of her. In the dream her hands were grasping, her flesh throbbed in a mountainous, heaving way, fermenting, saturated with moisture, folded into many voluptuous

layers. Bijou was always prone, inert, awakening only for
the moment of love. All the fluids of desire seeping along the
silver shadows of her legs, around the violin–shaped hips,
descending and ascending with a sound of wet silk around
the hollows of her breasts.

Elena imagined her everywhere, in the tight skirt
of the streetwalker, always preying and waiting. Pierre
had loved her obscene walk, her naïve glance, her drunken
sullenness, her virginal voice. For a few nights he had
loved that walking sex, that ambulant womb, open to all.

And now perhaps he loved her again.

Pierre showed Elena a photograph of his mother,
the luxuriant mother. The resemblance to Bijou
was startling in all but the eyes. Bijou's were cir–
cled with mauve. Pierre's mother had a
healthier air. But the body—

Then Elena thought, I am lost. She did not
believe Pierre's story that Bijou repulsed him now.
She began to frequent the café where Bijou and Pierre
had met, hoping for a discovery that would end her

doubts. She discovered nothing, except that Bijou liked very young men, fresh faced, fresh–lipped, fresh–blooded. That calmed her a little.

While Elena sought to meet Bijou and unmask the enemy, Leila was seeking to meet Elena, with ruses.

And the three women met, driven inside of the same café on a day of heavy rain: Leila, perfumed and dashing, carrying her head high, a silver fox stole undulating around her shoulders over her trim black suit; Elena, in a wine–colored velvet; and Bijou, in her street-walker's costume, which she could never abandon, the tight fitting black dress and high–heeled shoes. Leila smiled at Bijou, then recognized Elena. Shivering, the three sat down before apéritifs. What Elena had not expected was to be completely intoxicated with Bijou's voluptuous charm. On her right sat Leila, incisive, brilliant, and on her left, Bijou, like a bed of sensuality Elena wanted to fall into.

Leila observed her and suffered. Then she set about courting Bijou, which she could do

so much better than Elena. Bijou had never known women
like Leila, only the women who worked with her, who,
when the men were not there, indulged with Bijou in
orgies of kisses, to compensate for the brutality of the
men—sitting and kissing themselves into a hypnotic state,
that was all.

She was susceptible to Leila's subtle flattery, but
at the same time she was spellbound with Elena. Elena
was a complete novelty for her. Elena represented to men
a type of woman who was the opposite of the whore, a
woman who poetized and dramatized love, mixed it with
emotion, a woman who seemed made of another sub-
stance, a woman one imagined created by a legend. Yes,
Bijou knew men well enough to know this was also a
woman they were incited to initiate to sensuality, whom
they enjoyed seeing become enslaved by sensuality. The
more legendary the woman, the greater the pleasure in
desecrating, eroticizing her. Deep down, she was, under
all the dreaminess, another courtesan, living also for the
pleasure of man.

Bijou, who was the whore of whores, would have liked to exchange places with Elena. Whores always envy women who have the faculty of arousing desire and illusion as well as hunger. Bijou, the sex organ walking undisguised, would have liked to have the appearance of Elena. And Elena was thinking how she would have liked to change places with Bijou, for the many times when men grew tired of courting and wanted sex without it, bestial and direct. Elena pined to be raped anew each day, without regard for her feelings; Bijou pined to be idealized. Leila alone was satisfied to be born free of man's tyranny, to be free of man. But she did not realize that imitating man was not being free of him.

She paid her court suavely, flatteringly, to the whore of whores. As none of the three women abdicated, they finally walked out together. Leila invited Elena and Bijou to her apartment.

When they arrived, it was scented with burning incense. The only light came from illuminated glass globes filled with water and iridescent fish, corals and glass sea horses. This gave the room an undersea aspect, the appearance of a dream, a place where three diversely beautiful women exhaled such sensual auras that a man would have been overcome.

Bijou was afraid to move. Everything looked so fragile to her. She sat cross-legged like an Arab woman, smoking. Elena seemed to radiate light like the glass globes. Her eyes shone brilliant and feverish in the semidarkness. Leila emitted a mysterious charm for both women, an atmosphere of the unknown.

The three of them sat on the very low couch, on a heaving sea of pillows. The first one to move was Leila, who slid her jeweled hand under Bijou's skirts and gasped slightly with surprise at the unexpected touch of flesh where she had expected to find silky underwear. Bijou lay

back and turned her mouth towards Elena, her strength
tempted by the fragility of Elena, knowing for the first time
what it was to feel like a man and to feel a woman's
slightness bending under the weight of a mouth, the small
head bent back by her heavy hands, the light hair flying
about. Bijou's strong hands encircled the dainty neck with
delight. She held the head like a cup between her hands to
drink from the mouth long draughts of nectar breath, her
tongue undulating.

Leila had a moment of jealousy. Each caress she
gave to Bijou, Bijou transmitted to Elena—the very same
caress. After Leila kissed Bijou's luxuriant mouth,
Bijou took Elena's lips between hers. When Leila's
hand slipped further under Bijou's dress, Bijou slid
her hand under Elena's. Elena did not move, fill-
ing herself with languor. Then Leila
slid to her knees and used both hands
to stroke Bijou. When she pushed up
Bijou's dress, Bijou threw her
body back

and closed
her eyes to
better feel the movements of
the warm, incisive hands. Elena, seeing
Bijou offered, dared to touch her voluptuous body
and follow every contour of the rich curves—a bed
of down, soft, firm flesh without bones, smelling
of sandalwood and musk. Her own nipples hard-
ened as she touched Bijou's breasts. When her
hand passed around Bijou's buttocks, it met
Leila's hand.

Then Leila began to undress, exposing
a soft little black satin corselet, which held her
stockings with tiny black garters. Her thighs,
slender and white, gleamed, her sex lay in shadow. Elena
loosened the garters to watch the polished legs emerging.
Bijou threw her dress over her head and then leaned for-
wards to finish pulling it off, exposing as she did so the
fullness of her buttocks, the dimples at the bottom of the
spine, the incurving back. Then Elena slid out of her dress.

She was wearing black lace underwear that was slit open back and front, showing only the shadowy folds of her sexual secrets.

DANTE ALIGHIERI

Inferno

ROM

the first circle thus I passed below

> Down to the second, which less space doth bound,
>
> And keener pain, that goads to cries of woe.

There dreaded Minos stands and snarls around,

> And tries the crimes of those that enter in,
>
> Judges, and sends as he his tail hath wound.

I say that when the soul whom Hell doth win

Comes in his presence, all its guilt confessed,

And when that grand inquisitor of sin

Sees in what part of Hell that soul should rest,

He round his frame his mighty tail doth throw

As oft as he would fix its grade unblest.

Even in size the crowd before him grew,

And each in turn approaches and is tried;

They speak, they hear, and then are thrust below.

"O thou who to this hostel dark hast plied

Thy way," spake Minos, when he saw me there,

And for a time his great work put aside,

"How thou dost come, in whom dost trust, take care:

Let not the open entrance cheat thy soul."

Then spake my Guide: "What means this cry I hear?

Seek not his destined journey to control;

So is this willed where what is willed is one

(Ask thou no more) with might that works the whole."

Then to mine ears deep groans an entrance won,

Before unheard: I now had reached a spot

Where smote mine ear loud wail and many a groan.

I came unto a place where light was not,

Which murmurs ever like a storm-vext sea,

When strife of winds in conflict waxes hot.

That storm of Hell, which rest doth never see,

Bears on the spirits with its whirling blast,

And, hurling, dashing, pains exceedingly.

When they before the precipice have passed,

There pour they tears and wailing and lament,

There curses fierce at God's high power they cast.

And then I knew this pain did those torment

Who had in life been sinners carnally,

And bowed their reason to lust's blandishment.

And as the starlings through the winter sky

Float on their wings in squadron long and dense,

So doth that storm the sinful souls sweep by:

Here, there, up, down, it drives in wild suspense.

Nor any hope their agony allays,

Or of repose or anguish less intense.

And as the cranes fly chanting out their lays,

And in the air form into lengthened line,

So these I looked on wailing

went their ways,

Souls borne where fierce winds, as I

said, combine.

Wherefore I spake: "O Master,

who are these,

The people who in this dark

tempest pine?"

"The first of these," he said, "of whom

'twould please

Thy mind to hear, was once an empress famed

Of many peoples, nations, languages;

So sunk was she in foul lusts, evil-shamed,

That in her law she owned no rule but will,

That so her guilt might pass less sorely blamed.

Semiramis is she, whose record still

We read, who Ninus married and replaced:

She ruled the lands the Soldan's power doth fill.

The next is she who, by her love disgraced,

Sought death, unfaithful to Sichaeus dead.

Then Cleopatra, wanton and unchaste."

Then Helena I saw, whose beauty bred

Such evil times; the great Achilles too,

Who to the end in love's might combated.

Paris and Tristan, thousands more in view,

He, with his finger pointing, showed and named,

Whom love from this our earthly life withdrew.

And as I listened to my Teacher famed,

Telling of all those dames and knights of old,

I was as lost, and grief its victory claimed.

And I began: "O Poet, I am bold

To wish to speak awhile to yonder pair,

Who floated so lightly on the storm—blast cold."

And he to me: "Thou'lt see them when they fare

More near to us: then pray them by that love

That leads them: they will to thy call repair."

Soon as the winds their forms towards us move,

My voice I lift: "O souls sore spent and driven,

Come ye and speak to us, if none reprove."

And e'en as doves, when love its call has given,

    With open, steady wings to their sweet nest

    Fly, by their will borne onward through the heaven,

So from the band where Dido was they pressed,

    And came towards us through the air malign,

    So strong the loving cry to them addressed.

"O living creature, gracious and benign,

    Who com'st to visit, through the thick air perse,

    Us, whose blood did the earth incarnadine,

Were He our friend who rules the universe,

    We would pray Him to grant thee all His peace,

    Since thou has pity on our doom perverse.

Of that which thee to hear and speak shall please

    We too will gladly with thee speak and hear,

    While, as it chances now, the wild winds cease.

The land where I was born is situate there

    Where to the sea-coast line descends the Po,

    To rest with all that to him tribute bear.

Love, which the gentle heart learns quick to know,

    Seized him thou seest, for the presence fair

They

robbed me

of the mode still

deepens woe.

Love, who doth none beloved from loving spare,

Seized me for him with might that such joy bred,

That, as thou seest, it leaves me not e'en here.

Love to one death our steps together led;

Caïna him who quenched our life doth wait."

Thus was it that were borne the words

they said,

And when I heard those souls in sad estate,

I bowed my face, and so long kept it low,

Till spake the poet: "What dost meditate?"

When I made answer, I began, "Ah woe!

What sweet fond thoughts, what passionate desire

Led to the pass whence such great sorrows flow?"

Then I turned to them and began inquire,

"Francesca," so I spake, "thy miseries

A pitying grief that makes me weep inspire.

But tell me, in the time of those sweet sighs,

    The hour, the mode, in which love led you on

    Doubtful desires to know with open eyes."

And she to me: "A greater grief is none

    Than to remember happier seasons past

    In anguish: this thy Teacher well hath known:

But if thou seek'st to learn what brought at last

    Our love's first hidden root to open sight,

    I'll tell, as one who speaks while tears flow fast.

It chanced one day we read for our delight

    How love held fast the soul of Lancelot;

    Alone were we, nor deemed but all

    was right;

Full many a time our eyes their glances shot,

    As we read on; our cheeks now paled, now blushed;

    But one short moment doomed us to our lot.

When as we read how smile long sought for flushed

    Fair face at kiss of lover so renowned,

    He kissed me on my lips, as impulse rushed,

All trembling; now with me for aye is bound.

Writer and book were Gallehault to our will:

No time for reading more that day we found."

And while one spirit told the story, still

The other wept so sore, that, pitying, I

Fainted away as though my grief would kill,

And fell, as falls a dead man, heavily.

TERRY McMILLAN

Touching

SUSPECTED
someone was there in that *very* same spot before me,
but I didn't let the thought grow in my mind or rot
there, till I saw her swinging on your side like a shoul-
der–strap purse early this morning. And this was after
I had already let you touch me all over with your long
brown hands and break down my resistance, so that

you left me
feeling like the
earth had been pulled from
under my feet.

First, I see your lean long legs coming
toward me on that crooked gray sidewalk, the silver
specks glaring in my eyes like dancing stars. But I
was not blinded, even when you dragged them in
that elegant, yet pompous kinda way of yours. And
you watched me coming from at least a half a block
away and those size 13s didn't seem to lift off the
cement as high as they did the other night when
we walked down this *very* same street together.

I know it was me who called you up the
other night to say hello, but it was *you* who invited me to
come down and walk your dog with you. Sounded innocent
enough to me, but all along I'm sure you knew that I wanted
to finally find out how warm it was under your shirt, behind
your zipper, and if your hands were as gentle and strong as
they looked. I was really hoping we could skip the walk

altogether 'cause I just wanted to fall down on you slowly and get to your insides. Walk the dog another time. But since you could've misconstrued my motives as being unladylike, I bounced on down the street to your apartment in my white jogging outfit, trying to look as alluring as I possibly could, but without looking too eager.

I even dabbed gold oil behind my ears, under each breast and on the tips of my elbows so as to lure you closer to me in case you couldn't make up your mind. The truth of the matter is that I was nervous because I knew that we weren't gonna just chitchat tonight like we'd done before. I went out of my way in five minutes flat to brush my teeth twice, put on fresh coats of red lipstick, wash under my arms, Q-tip my ears and navel ('cause I didn't know just how far you might go), and wash my most intimate areas and sprinkle a little jasmine oil there too.

Even though it was almost ninety degrees, we walked fifteen blocks and the dog didn't let go of anything. You didn't seem to mind or notice. You handed me the leash, and even though I can't stand to see a grown man with a little cutesy-wutesy dog, I wasn't hostile as I tugged at it as we continued to walk through the thick night air. For the most part, I like dogs.

When our feet dropped from the curb, and I jumped and screamed because a fallen leaf looked like a dead mouse, I let go of the leash and grabbed your hand. You squeezed it back, though you had to drag me to chase after your dog, who had taken off down the sidewalk, running up to the tree's bark and just panting. When we finally caught him, we were both out of breath. I regretted wearing that sweaty jogging suit.

"You scared of a little mouse?" you asked.

"Yes, they give me the heebie-jeebies. My stomach turns over and I want to jump on top of chairs and stuff just to get away from them."

Then you told me about the time you busted one on

your kitchen counter eating your ravioli right out of the can and how you wounded it with a broomstick and then tried to flush it down the toilet, but it wouldn't flush. I laughed loud and hard, but I wanted to make you laugh, too.

So, I told you about the time I was on my way out of my house to take a sauna when I accidently saw a giant roach cavorting on my kitchen counter. I whacked it with my right hand just hard enough to cripple it. (I am scared of mice but I hate roaches.) I didn't want it to die immediately because I had just spent $9.95 on some Roach—Pruf which I had ordered through the newspaper and wanted to see if it *really* worked. So, I sprinkled about a quarter teaspoon on his head as he was about to struggle to find a crack or crevice somewhere. He kept on trying so I kept on sprin-kling more Pruf on his antennae. After five minutes of this, he was getting on my nerves 'cause I still had my coat on, my purse and gym bag thrown over my shoulders, and since my kitchen was designed strictly with dwarfs and children in mind, I was burning up. It was then that I decided to burn him up too. First I lit myself a cigarette, and with the same match, burned off his antennae but the sucker still kept trying to get to one corner of the counter. I got real mad because my Pruf was obviously not working and I just went ahead and burnt him up quickly and totally for not dying the way he was supposed to.

You thought this was terribly funny and cracked up. I liked hearing you laugh, but I didn't know if you thought this was indicative of my personality: torture and murder and everything.

We continued to walk a few more blocks, making small talk and the dog continued running up to tree trunks, kicking up his little white legs and finally squirting out wetness, but that was about it.

By this time, I was sweating and picturing your head nestled between my breasts. I like feeling a man's head there, and it had been so long since any man even made me feel like dreaming out loud that I didn't even hear you when you asked me if I liked the Temptations and had I ever been to a

puppet show.
I didn't understand
the connection until
we walked inside your apartment.
Today though, you watched me come toward you
like this was a tug-of-war, but the rope was invisible. The
gravity was so dense that it pulled us face to face and
when I finally reached you I could smell your breath at
the end of the rope. You were uneasy, and sorta turned
in a half-turn toward me as I brushed past both of you.
You loosely smiled back at me, squinting behind those
tinted glasses, and I smiled back at both of you 'cause I
don't have a grudge with this girl; wasn't *her* who I
spent the night with.

"What are *you* doing up so early?" you asked. I
didn't really think it was any of your business since you
didn't call last night to see how late I was up. Besides, it
was almost ten o'clock in the morning.

"I've already had my coffee, done my laundry, and
now I'm trying to get to the plant store to buy some dirt so

I can transplant my fern and rubber tree before the block party this afternoon."

"Oh, I'm sorry, Marie, this is Carolyn," you said, waving your hands between us like a magician.

We both nodded like ladies, fully understanding your uneasiness.

"Why don't you have the Chinese people do your laundry?" you asked.

"Because I like to know that my clothes are clean; I like to fold them up nice and neat like I want them. And besides, I like to put things together that belong together."

You just nodded your head like a fool. For a moment you looked puzzled, like someone had dropped you off in the middle of nowhere. You didn't seem to mind either that the girl was standing there watching your poise alter and sway. Me neither. But I had to move away from you 'cause I could really smell your body scent now and it was starting to stick to my skin, gravitating around me, until it got all up into my nostrils and then hit my brain, swelled up my whole head right there on the spot. This was embar-

rassing, so I tried to play it off by pulling my
scarlet scarf down closer toward my eye-
brows. But you already knew what had
happened.

I make my feet move away from you
as if I am trying to catch a bus I see approaching.
I take my hands and wipe away the burnt-red lip-
stick from my mouth and cheeks at the mere
thought of letting you press yours against them. Was trying
to forget how handsome you were altogether. Fine. Too
fine. Didn't listen to my mama. "Never look at a man that's
prettier than you, 'cause he's gonna act that way." I was
trying to think about dirt. The leaves of my plants. But I
never have been attracted to pretty men, I thought, trying to
miss the cracks in the sidewalk after stubbing my toe. You
were different. Spoke correct English. Made puppets move
and talk. Wrote your own grant proposals. Drank herbal
tea and didn't smoke cigarettes. You crossed your legs and
arms when you talked, and leaned your wide shoulders back
in your chair so your behind slid to the edge. Made me

think you thought about the words before letting them roll off your tongue. I admired you for contemplating things before you made them happen.

You yelled at me after I was almost halfway down the block. "Are you selling anything at the block party?"

I had already told you the other day I was making zucchini cake, but I repeated it again. "Zucchini cake!" and waved good-bye, trying to keep that stupid grin on my face though I knew you wouldn't have been able to see my expression from a distance.

I liked the attention you were giving me in spite of the girl. I thought it meant something. I was even hoping as I trucked into the plant store and got stuck by a cactus that you would call me later on to explain that she was just a friend of your cousin or your sister. I was hoping that you would tell me that your back hurt or something so I could come down with my almond oil and rub it for you. Beat it, dig my fingertips

into your shoulder blades and the canals along your spine
until you gave in. Or maybe you would tell me you broke
your glasses and couldn't see. I would come down and read
out loud to you: comic books or the Bible.

Now, I'm out here on this sidewalk with a bag of
black dirt in my hands in the heat walking past your house,
forcing myself not to stare up at those dingy white shutters
of yours so I twist my neck in the opposite direction, look-
ing ridiculous and completely conspicuous. I thought for
sure I was gonna be your one-and-only-down-the-street
sweetheart, 'cause I carried myself like a lady, not like some
dog in heat.

I really had no intention of transplanting anything
today. I just told you that because it sounded clean. I was
more concerned about whether this girl touched you last
night the way I had. Probably not, because only I can touch
you the way I touch you. But as you were standing there on
that sidewalk, I kept seeing still shots of us flashing across
my eyes: twisting inside each other's arms like worms and
caterpillars; you kissing me like you'd been getting paid for

it all these years
and this was your
last paycheck; and my head getting
lost all over your body. I could still hear your faint
cries echoing in my head right there on the concrete. Saw
my tongue moistening your chest and your hands rubbing
all across and around my back like I was made of silk. I
was silk and you knew it. You smelled so damn good.
And you never stopped me when my head fell off the
bed. You came after it. You never said anything when I
screamed and called out your name, just took your time
with me and kept pulling me inside your arms, inside
the cave of your chest and would not let me go. And
when I woke up, you were the dream I thought I had.

And yet, there you were out on that sidewalk in
the heat with another girl chained to your arm, walking
past my house without a care in the world. This shit
burns me up.

I mean, look. You didn't have to make me laugh out
loud, tickle me, and change the Band-Aid on my cut thumb,

or sniff my hair and tell me it smelled like a cool for-
est. You didn't have to tell me it didn't matter that my
breasts were small, and I was relieved to hear that,
'cause my mama always told me that a man
should be more interested in how you fill his life
and not how you fill your bra.

I mean, who told you to show me
the puppets you'd made of James Brown and
Diana Ross and the Jackson Five? Who told
you to burn jasmine candles and make me
listen to twelve old Temptations albums after
telling me your favorite one of all was "Ain't
Too Proud to Beg"? You didn't have to climb
up on a barstool and drag out your scrap-
book and give me the privilege of seeing
four generations of your family. Showing me
your picture as a little nappy-headed boy.
What made you think I wanted to see you as a child
when I'd really only known you as a man for three
weeks? But no, you watched me turn my key in my

front door for two whole months while you walked that little mutt before you allowed yourself to say more than "hello" and "good morning."

I never did get around to explaining myself, did it? I mean, I think I told you I was a special education teacher. I think I told you that once in a while I write poems. Even wrote one for you but I'm glad I didn't give it to you. Your ego probably would've popped out of your chest. But maybe I should've told you about the nights when my head pumps blood, and about the dreams I have of being loved just so. How I have always wanted to give a man more than sym—phony inside and outside the bedroom. But it is so hard. Look at this.

You just should not have wrapped your arms and shoulders around me like I was your firstborn child. You should not have shown me tenderness and passion. Was this just lust? I mean, I wasn't asleep when you kept on touching and rubbing my face like I was crystal and you were afraid I would break. I pretended because I didn't want you to rupture this cocoon I was inside of. So I just let you touch; never wanted you to stop touching me.

Three hours ago I transplanted my plant anyway. I baked three zucchini cakes that cost me almost thirty dollars, but after this morning I cannot picture myself sitting out on those cement steps in the heat trying to sell a piece of cake to total strangers. My roommate said she didn't mind. And I'm not going to sit in this hot house all day and be miserable.

"Wanna meet me for brunch?" I ask a girlfriend. She has no money. "I'll pay, just meet me, girl, okay?" She understands that I'm not really hungry but will eat anything just to take up inside space and get me away from this street.

The block was starting to fill up with makeshift vendors displaying junk they'd pulled out of attics and closets and basements so that they wouldn't have to drag them to the Salvation Army. I could already smell barbecue and popcorn and hear the d.j. testing his speakers for the highest quality of sound that he could expect to get from outside. It was very.

hot and the sun was beating down on the pavement, making the heat penetrate through your shoes.

I'm wearing my tightest bluejeans and think I look especially good this afternoon on my way to the train station. I work hard to look good. Not for you or for the general public, but for me. Here you come again, strutting toward me with that sissy little dog tagging alongside your big feet, but this time there's nothing on your arm but soft black hair and a rolled-up red plaid shirt sleeve. I can see orchards of black hair peeking out at me from your chest and though my knees want to buckle, I dig my heels deeply into the leather so as to make myself stand up straight like a dancer. You smile at me before we meet face to face and then do one of your about-face turns. Start walking beside me without even being invited.

"Hello," I say, as I make sure I don't lose the pace of my stride I've worked so hard on establishing when I first noticed you.

"My goodness,

119

you *do* look pretty today. Pink and purple are definitely your colors."

I smile because I know I look good and even though I can hardly breathe from holding my stomach in to look its absolute flattest, I don't want you staring at anything on my body too tough because you've seen far too much of it already. I take that back. I want you to be mesmerized by this sight so that you remember what everything looked and felt like underneath this denim because you won't be any-where near that close again: daytime or nighttime. I move closer to the curb.

"Where you going today?" you ask, showing some real interest. And since I want you to think I'm a very busy woman and that this little episode has not fazed me in the least, I say, "I'm having brunch with a friend." I really wanted to tell you it wasn't any of your damn business, but no, I'm not only polite, but honest.

We walked six hard hot blocks and when we finally reached the subway steps, you bent down like you were about to kiss me, and I stared at your smooth brown lips

puckering up
as if you had
a cold sore on
them, and turned my head.

You kissed that girl this morning.

    "Can I call you later, then?" you asked.

    "If the spirit moves you," I said and disappeared underground.

    By the time I got home it was almost ten o'clock and the street was still full of teenagers roller-skating, skateboarding, and dancing to the loud disco music blasting from both ends of the block. Kids were running around and through a full-spraying fire hydrant in high shrills of excitement, while grownups sat on the stoops sipping beers and drinks from Styrofoam cups. My roommate was sitting on our stoop and I joined her. Though it was hard to see, I found myself looking for your tall body over the smaller ones. When I didn't see you immediately, this disturbed me because I could see your lights on and I knew you couldn't be sitting up in that muggy apartment with all this noise and activity going on down here.

When I saw you leaning against a wrought-iron fence across the street, there was a different girl stuck deep into your side. You spotted me through the thick crowd of teenagers and I heard you call out my name, but I ignored you. I was too proud to let myself feel sad or jealous or anything stupid like that.

My roommate told me she sold exactly three pieces of my zucchini cake because folks were afraid to buy it. Thought it might be green inside. I didn't care about the loss.

I felt spry and spunky, so I kicked off my pink pumps and marched down the steps and walked straight into the fanning water of the fire hydrant along with the kids. The hard mist felt cool and soothing as it fell against my skin. My entire body was tingling as if I had just had a massage. And even though I could feel your eyes following me, I didn't turn to acknowledge them. I sat back down on the steps, wiped the water from my forehead, the hot pink lipstick from my lips, ate a piece of my delicious zucchini cake, and popped the lid on an ice-cold beer. The foam flowed over the top of the bottle and down my fingers. I shook off the excess, and leaned back against the cement steps so it would scratch my back when I rocked from side to side and popped my fingers to the beat.

AUTHOR BIOGRAPHIES

The Italian poet DANTE ALIGHIERI *penned the epic* Divine Comedy *in 1321. The first section,* The Inferno, *follows our narrator on a tour of hell, led by the poet Virgil. The grueling journey descends through nine twisting levels, each descending further into the bowels of the earth. On the way, Dante passes the second level, permanent home to lusters.*

CHARLES BAUDELAIRE *is more famous for decadent lifestyle than poetry. The romantic, swashbuckling Frenchman completed only one book of verse, the painfully sensuous* Fleur du Mal— *a profound foreshadowing of modern poetry. Unfortunately, Baudelaire paid for his fun; he died at forty-six in 1867.*

ITALO CALVINO'S *writings range from fantastical tales of the evolution of the universe (*Cosmicomics*) to prose poems by historical figures like Marco Polo (*Invisible Cities*).* If on a Winter's Night a Traveller *casts the reader as the protagonist in a series of novels that begin but never end. His last, spare novel,* Mr. Palomar *(1983), records the meditations of our hero throughout a variety of intriguing observations.*

SIMONE DE BEAUVOIR'S *1953 essay,* The Second Sex, *was a feminist call to arms: a full frontal attack on women's roles in society. The French philosopher, novelist, and essayist was a life-long partner of existentialist philosopher Jean-Paul Sartre.*

In 1949, Italian filmmaker and poet PIER PAOLO PASOLINI openly announced his homosexuality. The Italian Communist Party, with whom he worked for several years, promptly expelled him on charges of "moral and political unworthiness." Pasolini fled to Rome, where he lived in the impoverished outskirts of the city. He died under mysterious circumstances in 1975.

In his younger years, English poet JOHN DONNE'S fondness for women's company led to saucy, often satiric verse. Eventually however, he became an Anglican preacher and, predictably, his poems turned to dour themes, such as sin and death. While Donne was extremely popular during his lifetime, he fell into disapproval in the eighteenth century and has only recently resurfaced.

The frank eroticism of Jayadeva's Gitagovinda led seventeenth-century scholars to interpret the fiery Sanskrit love poems as an allegory of the human soul's love for God. But Indian readers were mesmerized by the longing of the separated lovers. To this day, in Bengal, Nepal, and India, the ever-popular Gitagovinda is sung in celebration of the coming Spring.

Czech novelist MILAN KUNDERA is the author of six genre-melding novels, blending Czech and Slovak political history, comic asides, essays on erotic matters, and good stories. His most popular book, The Unbearable Lightness of Being (1986), follows in essay and fiction the political and sexual exploits of Tomas, a blacklisted doctor.

Peruvian writer MARIO VARGAS LLOSA *is the author of ten novels,*
including The Storyteller, Aunt Julia and the Scriptwriter, *and*
The Cathedral. *None received more attention than 1990's controversial*
In Praise of the Stepmother. *As* Playboy *suggested, reading the book was*
"like floating in a pool on a warm day and having a long erotic daydream."

TERRY MCMILLAN *is the author of three novels,* Mama,
Disappearing Acts, *and* Waiting to Exhale, *and is the editor of*
Breaking Ice: Contemporary African American Fiction. *Her 1985*
short story "Touching" *was first published in the* Coydog Review.
McMillan currently lives outside San Francisco.

Upon its 1955 release, VLADIMIR NABOKOV's Lolita *was*
burned in France, banned in the United States, and hotly debated in British
Parliament. The author defended his tale of a middle aged man's sexual
obsession with 9– to 14–year–old girls as strictly moral, not obscene.

The darkly erotic Twenty Love Poems and a Song of Despair *(first pub–*
lished in Santiago de Chile in 1924, English translation copyright 1969) estab–
lished PABLO NERUDA *as one of Chile's most promising writers.*
But this writer would not rest on his laurels; he went on to publish dozens of
volumes of poetry and prose, many of the later ones with a decidedly Socialist
bent. Neruda won the Nobel Prize for Literature in 1971.

A compulsive chronicler of her very private life, ANAÏS NIN *is best known for her seven-volume* Diaries 1931–1974, *which detail her bohemian life in Paris and New York, as well as her notorious affair with Henry Miller. Nin also published two books of erotica,* Little Birds *and* Delta of Venus, *from which this excerpt is taken.*

Desperate blood-lust suffuses all four of ANNE RICE's *widely-read* The Vampire Chronicles. *The author is no stranger to carnal passions, which fill many of her novels, including* Cry to Heaven *and* The Witching Hour, *as well as the erotica published under one of her pseudonyms, A. N. Roquelaure.*

The fragments of SAPPHO's *passionate love poems date to 600 B.C. It was on the isle of Lesbos where this mysterious writer tutored a cult of young girls in the arts. Legend has it that she flung herself into the sea in the throes of unrequited love.*

ACKNOWLEDGMENTS

Excerpt from *In Praise of the Stepmother* by Mario Vargas Llosa © 1988 by Mario Vargas Llosa.
English translation © 1990 by Farrar, Straus and Giroux. Reprinted by
permission of Farrar, Straus and Giroux.

"Lightness and Weight" from *The Unbearable Lightness of Being* by
Milan Kundera © 1985 by Milan Kundera. English translation copyright © 1985 by HarperCollins
Publishers. Reprinted by permission of HarperCollins Publishers.

Excerpts from *Jayadeva's Gitagovinda,* edited and translated
by Barbara Stoler Miller © 1977 by Columbia University Press. Reprinted by permission
of Columbia University Press.

"The Loves of the Tortoises" from *Mr. Palomar* by Italo Calvino © 1983
by Giulio Einardi editore s.p.a., Torino. English translation copyright © 1985 by Harcourt Brace &
Company. Reprinted by permission of Harcourt Brace & Company.

Excerpt from *The Prime of Life, The Autobiography 1929–1944* by
Simone de Beauvoir © 1991 by HarperCollins Publishers. Reprinted by permission
of HarperCollins Publishers.

Excerpts from *Roman Poems* by Pier Paolo Pasolini © 1986 by City Lights Books. Translated
by Lawrence Ferlinghetti and Francesca Valente. Reprinted by permission of City Lights Books.

Excerpt from *Lolita* by Vladimir Nabokov © 1955 by Vladimir Nabokov.
Reprinted by permission of Vintage Books, a division of Random House, Inc.

Excerpt from *The Vampire Lestat* by Anne Rice © 1985 by Anne O'Brien Rice.
Reprinted by permission of Alfred A. Knopf, Inc.

Charles Baudelaire's "Afternoon Song" © 1993 by Randall Koral
and Ruth Marshall.

"Drunk with Pines" from *Twenty Love Poems and a Song of Despair* by
Pablo Neruda © 1969 by W.S. Merwin. Reprinted by permission of Penguin USA.

Excerpt from "Elena" in *Delta of Venus, Erotica* by Anaïs Nin © 1977 by
The Anaïs Nin Trust. Reprinted by permission of Harcourt Brace & Company.

"Touching" by Terry McMillan © 1985 by Terry McMillan. Reprinted by
permission of the author.